This book belongs to

_____

My dreams of hope are soaring – thank you Mum and Dad.
For my special dreamers T & J. ~ N

For my Mother and Father who have continually
been supportive of my work. ~ G

Text copyright © 2011 by Navjot Kaur
Illustrations copyright © 2011 by Gurleen Rai

First Edition 2011
2 4 6 8 10 9 7 5 3 1
Digit on the right indicates the number of this printing

This book was typeset in Garamond, Garamond Alternate and Mrs. Eaves
The illustrations were prepared using ink and gouache on board
Book design by Eulie Lee. www.eilue.com

Library and Archives Canada Cataloguing in Publication
Kaur, Navjot
    Dreams of hope : a bedtime lullaby / by Navjot Kaur ; illustrated by Gurleen Rai.
    ISBN 978-0-9812412-1-0
    1. Lullabies, English. I. Rai, Gurleen, 1985- II. Title.
PZ7.K16Dr 2011   j821'.92   C2010-903879-7

Printed and bound in Hong Kong
This book is printed on paper that is 100% recycled and processed chlorine-free.

Saffron Press
Visit us at www.saffronpress.com

Dreams of Hope

A Bedtime Lullaby

by Navjot Kaur

illustrated by Gurleen Rai

A lunar haze lights up the night,
Little One.

Glittering sitaray twinkle bright,
Little One.

Where will
our dream journey begin tonight,
Little One?

Close your eyes now, and just imagine,
Little One.

Dreams of hope flutter,

s w a y,

tickle your ears,

Little One.

Catch some and hold them dear,

Little One.

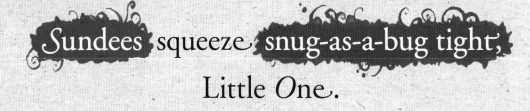

Sundees squeeze snug-as-a-bug tight,
Little One.

Soon, they will spread their wings and take flight,
Little One.

Chirus snuggle into their Shahtooshi, Little One.

Mountain top wheels spread mantras of kushi, Little One.

Deep oceans sing
healing lohreeyan,
Little One.

Mother Earth is
whispering messages of peace,
Little One.

Your gentle breaths echo deep in my heart,
Little One.

I love you.

Cuddle close, you are safe with me,
Little One.

Tonight is calm and quiet,
Little One.

Dreams of hope kiss you goodnight,
Little One.

Together, we will see what tomorrow brings,
Little One.

Glossary & Pronunciation Guide

Chiru • *Chee-roo*

A Tibetan antelope native to the Plateau region; considered endangered due to commercial poaching for its wool.

Kushi • *Ku-sh-ee* (In Panjabi: ਖੁਸ਼ੀ)

Happiness

Lohreeyan • *Loh-ree-aahn* (In Panjabi: ਲੋਰੀਆਂ)

Lullabies

Mantra • *Man-th-raa*

A sound, syllable, word or group of words that are thought to create spiritual peace

Shahtoosh • *Shah-too-sh*

A Chiru's wool; the fine underlayer close to the antelope's skin. Often made into shawls which are so fine they can pass through a ring. Unfortunately the Chirus are hunted for this purpose.

Sitaray • *See-taa-ray* (In Panjabi: ਸਿਤਾਰੇ)

Stars

Sundee • *Soo-n-d-ee* (In Panjabi: ਸੁੰਡੀ)

Caterpillar

Vaa hey guroo • *Vaa-hey-gu-roo*

The Gur Mantra used by Sikhs; Vaa or Vaahey is an expression of awe or wonder, gu means darkness and roo means light

My dreams of hope for you

Dreams of Hope Travel Guide

Dröm sött
Dream sweetly •
Sweden

8

Usv'i
Pronounced
"oosUH'ee"
Goodnight •
Cherokee

1

2

3

**Twinkle, twinkle
little star**
Britain

6

9

Dulces sueños
Sweet dreams •
Spain

7

Fatlı rüyalar
Sweet dreams •
Turkey

4

Sogni d'oro
Golden
dreams • Italy

Mira la luna
Mexican lullaby

10

**Que sueñes con
los angelitos**
May you dream with the
little angels • Argentina

5

11

**Ubusuku
obuhle
namaphupho
amamnandi**
Good night and
sweet dreams •
Zulu

Atlantic

Paci
Ocea